MONSTER By Mistake!

Tracy's Jacket

Adapted by **Paul Kropp**

Based on the screenplay by
Deborah Jarvis

Graphics by **Studio 345**

WINDING
STAIR
PRESS

Monster By Mistake
Theme Song

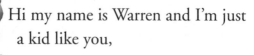

Hi my name is Warren and I'm just
a kid like you,

Or I was until I found evil
Gorgool's magic Jewel.

Then he tricked me and I read
a spell, now every
time I sneeze,

Monster By
Mistake…

My sister Tracy tries the
Spell Book.

She never gets it right.

But Tracy doesn't ever give
up, 'cause you know one day
she might

Find the words that will
return me to my former width
and height.

I'm a Monster By Mista....ah....ah...

I'm gonna tell you 'bout Johnny the
    Ghost,

He's a wisecracking,
    trumpet playing
    friend.

He lives up in the
attic (shhh...Mom and
Dad don't know)

Johnny always has
    a helping hand
    to lend.

My secret Monster-iffic life always keeps
    me on the run.

And I have a funny
    feeling that the
    story's just begun.

Everybody thinks it's
    pretty awesome
    I've become

A Monster By Mistake!

I'm a Monster By Mistake!

I'm a Monster By Mistake!

Monster by Mistake
Text © 2002 by Winding Stair
Graphics © 2002 by Monster by Mistake Enterprises Ltd.
Monster By Mistake Created by Mark Mayerson
Produced by CCI Entertainment Ltd. and Catapult Productions
Series Executive Producers: Arnie Zipursky and Kim Davidson

National Library of Canada Cataloging in Publication Data

Kropp, Paul, 1948-
  Tracy's jacket

(Monster by mistake ; 5)
Based on an episode of the television program, Monster by mistake.
ISBN 1-55366-214-8

I. Jarvis, Deborah, 1954– . II. CCI Entertainment Ltd. III. Title.
IV. Title: Monster by mistake (Television program) V. Series:
Kropp, Paul, 1948– . Monster by mistake ; 5.

PS8571.R772T73 2002   jC813'.54   C2002-900354-7
PZ7.K93Tr 2002

Winding Stair Press
An imprint of Stewart House Publishing Inc.
290 North Queen Street, #210
Etobicoke, Ontario, M9C 5K4 Canada
1-866-574-6873

Executive Vice President and Publisher: Ken Proctor
Director of Publishing and Product Acquisition: Susan Jasper
Copy Editing: Martha Campbell
Text Design: Laura Brady
Cover Design: Darrin Laframboise

This book is available at special discounts for bulk purchases by
groups or organizations for sales promotions, premiums, fundraising
and educational purposes. For details, contact: Stewart House
Publishing Inc., Special Sales Department, 195 Allstate Parkway,
Markham, Ontario L3R 4T8. Toll free 1-866-474-3478.

1 2 3 4 5 6   07 06 05 04 03 02

Printed and bound in Canada

COLLECT THEM ALL

8 BOOKS SO FAR!

Contents

Chapter 1

It wasn't that Tracy Patterson was all that interested in boys. She was only twelve, after all, and most of the boys at Pickford Elementary School were losers. But then there was Darryl – "tall, dark and handsome," as her mother would say. "Oh so hot!" as Tracy's friends described him.

But somehow Darryl was talking to Tracy right outside her locker. She knew her friends were watching the two of them. She knew they must be dying of jealousy.

"So did you see *Kung Fu Revenge* yet?" asked Darryl. "It's *so* excellent!"

"Oh yeah," Tracy replied. "I rented it, like, just last night. It was great!"

Tracy smiled, trying to hide her crush on the boy. At the same time, she wanted to get up the nerve to ask him to the big school dance that was coming up.

"That has to be my favorite movie, ever," said Darryl.

"The best part was when the kung fu master turned out to be a woman," Tracy told him. "And then she chopped the evil king's sword in half."

"Yeah, that was really cool!" Darryl imitated the move, chopping his hand down with a loud *hi-ya*!

Tracy decided to follow suit and chopped down, too.

"*Hi-yaaah!*" she yelled.

Unfortunately, she chopped with the hand that was holding her math textbook. The book slammed down on Darryl's foot.

"Aaaggh!" Darryl cried out in pain.

"Oh no!" cried Tracy. "I'm so sorry. I didn't mean to do that."

"It's okay," said Darryl. "It doesn't hurt that much." He bent over to pick up the textbook. When Tracy bent over at the same time, their heads smashed together with a small thud.

"Ow!" shouted Darryl. "All right, Tracy, I surrender!"

Tracy blushed bright red. "I'm so sorry . . . again!"

What am I doing? She thought to herself. Darryl's going to think I'm a total klutz!

Actually, Darryl was thinking about the pain in his foot. He quickly grabbed the book off the floor before Tracy could do more damage. Then he handed it to her and winked. "Maybe you should put that weapon away."

"Thanks," said Tracy, taking the book and putting it out of harm's way. "So are you going with anybody to the, uh, dance tomorrow?"

"Oh, maybe," Darryl said. "You know anybody who wants to go?"

"Well, I kind of thought . . . " but before Tracy could finish, her friend Susan came gliding down the hall.

Tracy and Susan were two opposites. Tracy was a bit skinny and a bit awkward. She had blonde hair and a face that could only be described as "cute." Susan, on the other hand, was dark and exotic looking. She was graceful, artistic and interesting. And she, too, had a crush on the handsome Darryl.

"Oh hi, you two," Susan said. "Sorry I'm late, Darryl. I was practicing some new moves I made up for the dance."

Darryl seemed to take notice. "You make up your own dance moves?" he asked.

"Oh, of course," replied Susan. "I take ballet classes, you know. But this time I'm working on something special for the dance. Like this."

Susan began gracefully whirling and twirling around the hall of the school. Her dancing really was quite graceful and artistic. It was enough to make Tracy grit her teeth with envy.

"That's so awesome!" said Darryl. He was definitely impressed.

"By the way, have you decided who you're going with to the dance?" Susan asked. She did a quick twirl and ballet curtsy.

"Oh, I think I know," Darryl said. "I'm just working up my courage to ask her."

"Oh, you shouldn't worry," Susan cooed. "Every girl in school is just dying to go to the dance with you."

Susan and Darryl walked away together. Poor Tracy watched them go, her heart sinking. Compared to Susan, she felt like she didn't even exist.

Chapter 2

Tracy and Warren were on their way home from school. Tracy had just finished telling her eight-year-old brother about what had happened. She told him how Susan seemed to get all Darryl's attention.

"So what?" said Warren. "They're both on the school dance committee, aren't they?"

"Yeah, but you don't get it."

"What is it then?"

"Well, nobody asked me to be on the dance committee." Tracy kicked the ground. "Of course, why would they? I'm such a klutz."

"Tracy!" said Warren, surprised that his sister was being so hard on herself. "You're not a klutz!"

"Well, I sure feel that way around Susan! She's graceful and pretty. She can even speak French."

"I bet her fancy ballet moves will just seem dumb at the dance." Warren did a funny impression, shaking his hips, legs and arms all over the place. Tracy didn't even smile.

"I'm too dull to do even that much." Tracy sighed.

"You are not!" Warren was really getting worried about his sister. She needed a little boost of self-confidence. "You're smart and funny and know a lot about, well, everything!"

"Thanks for trying to cheer me up, Warren. But you're even more interesting than I am. At least you can turn into a monster."

That was true, of course. Because of a mistake with a certain magic spell, Warren turned into a large blue monster whenever he sneezed. But Tracy was the one who knew how to work the magic. She had used the Jewel of Fenrath and Book of Spells to do all sorts of tricks. The only thing she hadn't figured out was how to stop Warren from turning into the monster.

Warren was about to point all that out when Tracy gasped. "Oh, Warren! Look!"

Tracy was nearly drooling on the window of a fancy clothing store. There in the window was a leather jacket to die for. Shiny and black, the jacket had metal clasps up the front and flames stitched around the collar. It had style and flair and design – everything that Tracy wanted!

"That jacket is so amazing!" cried Tracy. "I think it's even my size."

"But you don't wear clothes like that," Warren pointed out.

Tracy looked stubborn. "Well, why not? I *should* be wearing great clothes. If I showed up at the dance wearing something that cool, then no one would think I was a klutz. It wouldn't even matter that I can't dance!"

Warren just shook his head. "Tracy, you're plenty cool just the way you are."

Tracy took no notice of his comment. "I just love it! Let's go in and find out how much it costs." She grabbed Warren's arm and dragged him into the store.

Chapter 3

As soon as Warren and Tracy got home, Tracy went right to her mother. Mrs. Patterson was in the living room doing her daily exercises. Tracy told her all about the jacket.

"So," said Tracy's mom, "this jacket you want is $300?"

Tracy was hopeful. "If you could maybe lend me the money, I could pay you back out of what I earn babysitting. With interest!"

"You'd have to babysit every child in Pickford for the rest of your life."

"But, Mom . . . "

Mrs. Patterson quickly finished her exercise routine. "I'm sorry, honey, but you really don't need a new jacket. What's wrong with your jean jacket?"

"I always wear that one," sighed Tracy.

"Then you can borrow something of mine," suggested her mother.

"No!" Tracy screamed. "Anything but that!" In despair, she ran off to her room.

Mrs. Patterson turned to Warren. "Was it something I said?" she asked him.

"It's being an almost-teenager, Mom," Warren told her. "They say she'll grow out of it."

Fifteen minutes later, Tracy was still moping on her bed. Warren had sneezed and turned into the Monster – a large blue, but very friendly monster. Now the Monster and Johnny the Ghost were doing their best to cheer her up. Johnny had been living with Warren and Tracy ever since his own house had fallen down. This time they were playing their trumpets, a Dixieland jazz number. The song came to an end, and Tracy was still down in the dumps.

"Concert's over, kid," said Johnny, floating just behind the young girl.

"Sorry, Johnny. That was really good. Very uplifting," Tracy sighed.

"You're still not feeling any better, are you?" asked the Monster.

"Oh, sure I am," said Tracy. But she wasn't fooling anyone.

"You know, Tracy," offered Johnny, "three hundred bucks is a lot of moolah."

"Moolah?" the Monster asked.

"Money, bucks, smackeroos!" Johnny explained. "Besides, it's not what you wear that matters, it's who you are inside."

Tracy hopped up from the bed. "That's what everyone says! But the me inside is just boring and I just want to look special. I want to look like someone who's unpredictable. Someone who can do anything!"

Tracy spotted the Book of Spells and the Jewel of Fenrath on her desk. Her eyes lit up hopefully.

"Wait a minute," she said. "Why didn't I think of this before?" Tracy picked up the book and jewel. "If I can't afford to buy that store jacket, I can create my own jacket with these!"

Johnny swooped down to where Tracy stood. "Wait a minute," he said, worried already. "You're going to use magic to make a jacket?"

"Of course!" said Tracy, smiling widely. "It worked for Cinderella, didn't it?"

"Tracy, that's a fairy tale!" the Monster pointed out."

"You shouldn't use the Jewel of Fenrath for stuff like this," Johnny told her.

"Besides, you don't really know what you're going to get," warned her brother. "Your magic is a little unpredictable. No offense."

Tracy danced happily to the middle of the room. "So what? Life is unpredictable. The new Tracy is going to be totally unpredictable. She'll be magnificent! Stand back, you guys!"

The Monster and Johnny stood as far back from Tracy as they could.

"*Ich stem nimoy flannigan ria nont!*" Tracy chanted.

The jewel began glowing bright blue, turning itself around in Tracy's hand.

"Racoota ultra chica, stitches para tont!"

The jewel bounced to the floor and zapped Tracy with blue lightning. Suddenly, she was completely surrounded by blue electricity.

Johnny and Warren were both worried, but the glow faded as quickly as it came. Tracy was unharmed, but the magic spell had definitely worked.

Tracy was now wearing a stylish black leather jacket. It was much like the one she had seen at the store – but even nicer.

"Oh, wow!" Tracy cried as she checked herself out in the mirror. "It's perfect!"

"That's some jacket, all right," said Johnny. "I haven't seen anything that nice since Rita Hayworth in *Cover Girl.*"

"Who?" the Monster asked.

"Oh, just a glamorous movie star back in my day," Johnny said.

"Thanks," Tracy told him. "Glamorous is good. This jacket makes me feel so . . . so special."

"It fits you perfectly," said the Monster.

Tracy turned enough to see the back of the jacket. "Look at that design on the back!" she cried.

Stitched into the leather was a picture of a girl made with gold thread.

"It's funny. The picture sort of looks like you," said Johnny.

He and the Monster both stared at the very life-like girl on the jacket.

Tracy felt incredibly happy. "That's because this jacket was made for me! It's unique, special, one of a kind!" Tracy struck a modeling pose. "And now, so am I!"

Chapter 4

Night came and passed, and the Patterson kids left for a new day of school. Of course, Tracy was wearing her new jacket. Throwing open the doors to Pickford Elementary School, Tracy strutted down the hallway. The stylish jacket gave her a whole new attitude.

Passing by the school gym, Tracy spotted Darryl practicing his basketball skills. As she entered the gym, he nailed a layup.

"Oh, hello, Darryl." Tracy said. Even her voice seemed deeper and a bit more interesting.

"Hey, Tracy," said Darryl, picking up the ball. "Wow, cool jacket!"

Tracy smiled. "Thanks. It's new."

Darryl looked at her with new eyes. "It's excellent! Makes you look . . . uh, well, different."

"Oh, really? How? More exciting, maybe?" Tracy was fishing for a compliment, but Darryl didn't take the bait.

"Yeah, sort of, maybe," replied Darryl.

"So is everything ready for the dance?" asked Tracy.

"Yeah, my dad's bringing the sound system in after class. We're turning the whole gym into a disco! We've even got one of those disco balls."

"Oh, cool!"

Darryl thought for a moment. "You want to come early and help us set up?"

"Me?" Tracy tried to stay calm and not sound too eager. "I guess I could probably make it."

"Great!" said Darryl. "Hey, heads up!" He tossed Tracy the basketball.

Tracy stumbled backwards trying to hold on to the ball. "Oh . . . I'm not that athletic. I could never . . ."

Suddenly, Tracy's arm shot forward and she began to dribble the ball like a pro. She bounced the ball from one hand to the other, between her legs, then rolled the ball along the length of her shoulders.

"Whoa!" said Darryl in surprise.

Still dribbling the ball, Tracy took off down the gym towards the basket. When she was close enough, she leapt through the air, spinning in a full circle before slam-dunking the ball in the net.

Darryl caught up with Tracy and picked up the ball. He looked at her, amazed. "How'd you do that?"

Tracy was a little out of breath, and probably even more shocked than Darryl. But she still tried to play it cool. "Oh, you know . . . just practice."

"You've got to be kidding!" Darryl said as the school bell rang for class. "Well, I guess I'll see you before the dance, eh?"

"I'll be there," Tracy called as Darryl ran out of the gym.

Then Tracy paused for a moment. "That was a good question, though," she said, talking to herself. Tracy didn't play basketball and had never learned how to dribble. So how did she do what she just did?

No answer came to mind, so Tracy shrugged and went off to class.

What Tracy couldn't see was the girl on the back of her jacket. The stitched

image of the girl had changed. Now it had a very sinister smile on its face.

Chapter 5

At noon, Warren was busy helping his mother make snacks. Mrs. Patterson ran a monthly book club and wanted to be ready for her guests.

Warren was getting bored. "Why are we making so much food, anyway?"

"Oh, you wouldn't believe how much food these women can eat. The sandwiches just seem to disappear," explained his mother.

While her back was turned, Johnny the Ghost swooped down and grabbed one of the sandwiches. He winked at Warren, then began munching.

"Hmm," said Mrs. Patterson when she looked back at the cutting board. "I swear there were more sandwiches here just a second ago."

Tracy entered the kitchen, smiling happily. "Hi, Mom!" she called.

"Hi, Tracy." Mrs. Patterson turned and stared at Tracy. Seeing the jacket, she gave her daughter a stern look. "Where did you get that jacket, young lady?"

"Isn't it great?" asked the girl.

"You didn't buy it, did you?"

"Of course not! I . . . uh . . . borrowed it," said Tracy.

Mrs. Patterson looked suspicious, but turned back to her task.

"Chill out, Mom. Don't blow your top," came Tracy's voice.

This was unusual since Tracy never spoke to her mom like that. It was *especially* unusual since Tracy hadn't even opened her mouth.

"What was that?" Tracy's mother asked as she turned around.

Tracy looked a little stunned herself. "It was nothing!" she squeaked.

"I hope not, young lady."

Then the voice came again. "Maybe you're starting to lose it, Mom!" Tracy slapped her hands over her mouth, but even that didn't stop the voice. Before her mother could reply, Tracy ran out of the kitchen to her room.

Mrs. Patterson looked at Warren. "Is there something wrong with your sister?"

Warren was just as puzzled as his mother. "She's almost a teenager, Mom," was all he could say. As if that really explained everything.

After Warren had finished helping his mother, he joined Tracy in the bedroom. Johnny, who had taken a few more sandwiches, was already beside her.

"How come you talked to Mom like that?" Warren asked.

"I didn't say a thing," Tracy replied.

"Yeah, right," Warren replied. "Keep it up and you'll be grounded for sure."

"But I didn't say anything," Tracy whined.

"I heard you!" Warren repeated.

"I didn't say anything at all," said Tracy. She was upset that her brother didn't believe her.

"I'm afraid I heard it, too," added Johnny. "Have any other weird things happened since you put that jacket on?"

"No!" said Tracy, loudly. "Well, not exactly."

"What does that mean?" asked Johnny.

"Nothing. Just forget it for now," Tracy blurted out. "I have to go. I promised

I would get to school early to help out."

Tracy walked over to the window and pushed it open with a grunt. To the shock of Warren and Johnny, she stepped out over the sill and began climbing down the side of the house.

"We've got a front door, you know,"

called Johnny, but it was too late to stop her.

As Tracy reached the sidewalk, Warren and Johnny got a clear view of the image on the back of the jacket. The face was moving. It seemed to be mouthing some words – "Girls just wanna have fun!" And then it winked.

Warren and Johnny gasped.

"That coat is alive!" cried Warren.

Johnny was ready to move. "We've got to stop her. Let's go!"

Chapter 6

Tracy zoomed all the way to school and was walking across the playground. Then she slowed suddenly, wondering why she had left her house by going out the window.

Tracy was startled out of her thoughts when Susan appeared.

"Hey, Tracy!" she said.

"Oh, hi, Susan," replied Tracy, starting towards the school doors.

"You look amazing! I mean, I love that jacket. Is it from Paris or what?"

"It might be. I don't know." Tracy said. She was feeling a little strange.

"It must say on the label. Let me check for you," offered Susan.

Before Susan could lay a finger on the jacket, Tracy zipped inside the school. She

slammed the door shut and locked it tight. Susan was stuck outside.

The face on the jacket muttered, "That'll teach Miss Nosy Face."

But Tracy didn't hear the voice. Nor did she know why she'd just locked her friend out in the cold. It was as if her body was just out of control.

Susan shook the door handles. "Tracy! Hey, Tracy, that's not funny! Let me in!"

Tracy ignored her. She began walking towards the gym – but then something really strange began to happen.

Tracy walked like she was being pushed – into lockers, up against doors, right down the hall. She was like a leaf being blown by the wind.

In the gym, a few teachers and a handful of students were busy preparing for the dance. Mr. Petrie was doing his best to hang a giant mirrored disco ball from the ceiling. When he finally got the ball attached, he climbed down the ladder to admire his work.

"All right! It's perfect!"

The gym was getting fixed up nicely for the dance. Ms. Gish was getting a table ready with drinks and snacks. Darryl was off in a corner setting up his dad's sound system.

Suddenly, Tracy flew through the

doors of the gym and fell to the floor. The teachers and students all stared at her.

"Uh, hi," said Tracy meekly.

"Are you all right?" asked Mr. Petrie.

Tracy stood up and dusted herself off. "I'm fine, thanks. Just making an entrance, as they say."

Mr. Petrie shrugged and moved on to his next task. Tracy walked over to where Darryl was working on the sound system.

"Wow," she said to him. "This equipment sure looks impressive."

Darryl was a total nut when it came to sound equipment. "It's a 1400 cc with active tracking and double subwoofers," he said proudly.

"Want to try that again, buddy, maybe in *English*?" said Tracy's voice. Tracy gasped, hearing her voice speak – though she wasn't talking.

Darryl turned to look at her. "Pardon?"

Tracy tried not to panic. "Um, what I mean is . . . can I help you with anything?"

"Uh, sure," he said. "Hold this."

Darryl handed Tracy a black box with cables coming out of it in all directions. He put on a set of headphones and plugged it into the box. Then Darryl leaned over to a nearby microphone and spoke into it.

"Testing, testing!" Darryl's voice was incredibly loud. It was loud enough to make old Ms. Gish jump, and she was at the other side of the gym.

Standing upright, Darryl turned back to Tracy. "Looks like the amp works. By the way, have you seen Susan yet?"

"Why are you interested in that show-off?" said the voice. The voice sounded exactly like Tracy, but it wasn't her! All Tracy could do was clap her hands over her mouth.

"What was that?" Darryl asked.

"I mean, Susan must be around some-where, I think," said Tracy. Suddenly, she felt warm. Tracy didn't know if it was the heat of the gym or her own embarrassment. "Gosh, it's hot in here."

"Why don't you take off your jacket?" Darryl suggested. "The coat rack is right over here."

Darryl put out his hand to guide Tracy, but when his fingers brushed the jacket he was zapped by blue electricity. He quickly jerked his hand away.

"Ow! Your jacket shocked me!" said Darryl. He shook his hand in pain.

"Uh, that's because it's from Paris," Tracy said. "Clothes have more static in France."

"Uh, right," Darryl said. Somehow he must have missed that particular lesson in science.

He went off to help Mr. Petrie set up a microphone.

As Darryl walked away, Tracy became aware that something was wrong. Terribly wrong. At home, she'd jumped out of a window. Here at school, she'd locked her best friend outside. And now the jacket had given Darryl an electric shock. And most of all, where was that voice – the one that sounded like her – coming from?

Chapter 7

Susan was still outside waiting for someone, anyone, to come along. Finally, it was Warren who approached. He was walking along with his invisible friend Johnny floating overhead.

"How come you're stuck out here?" asked Warren. "I thought you were helping to get ready for the dance."

"I'm locked out!" Susan replied, her voice near tears. "Tracy went in just ahead of me and must have locked the door by accident."

The invisible Johnny muttered to himself, "Either an accident, or the jacket did it."

Warren tried to be helpful. "Maybe I can get you inside," he offered.

"You?" laughed Susan. "You're only eight years old."

As she giggled, Johnny floated through the door and unlocked it from the inside. Susan couldn't see him, but the ghost momentarily became visible and winked at Warren. Then he became invisible again.

Warren smiled at Susan and walked up to the door. He turned the handle and opened it with ease.

"There you go," Warren said. "You know, sometimes us eight-year-olds can be quite surprising. It never pays to underestimate people."

Looking a little puzzled, Susan shook her head and entered the school. Warren followed close behind. Both of them headed for the gym.

In the gym, everything was just about ready to go for the dance. All that was left was for Darryl to connect the main power.

"Are you ready?" Darryl asked.

Mr. Petrie nodded, so Darryl moved to his equipment and pushed a single button. The lights of the gym dimmed, the music began, and the disco ball slowly started to spin. Colored lights were placed around the gym aimed at the ball. As it turned, little flashes of reflected light danced on the walls.

"Yes!" Tracy sighed.

"It works!" Darryl shouted over the music. The two of them did a high-five.

That was also the moment that Susan and Warren burst in through the doors. They both stopped in their tracks and admired the scene.

"Oh," said Susan, almost in a trance. "It's just perfect!"

Susan wasted no time in rushing to where Darryl and Tracy were talking. She grabbed the boy's hand and dragged him onto the dance floor.

"Let's dance!" cried Susan as she pulled Darryl along.

Tracy stood and watched them. Then she heard a voice speaking to her over the music. "Don't let her get away with that!" the voice said.

"What?" Tracy asked, speaking to no one she could see.

"Get out there, girl!" ordered the voice. "Show that guy how you can dance!"

Tracy was pushed along to where her friends were dancing. Once she was at the center of the floor, she, too, began to dance. Not just any dance, though. Tracy's arms and legs swung around wildly. She began dancing faster and faster, almost out of control.

"Tracy?" said Susan in disbelief.

"I'm a disco . . . maniac!" Tracy cried.

Even the teachers were staring at Tracy now. Finally, she stopped going wild and began doing some salsa moves to go with the music. Twisting and turning and even shaking her hips, Tracy burned up the dance floor.

Warren couldn't believe that this was his sister. Jacket or no jacket, Tracy would never be as wild as this.

Suddenly, a bolt of blue lightning came from the jacket. It zapped upwards and hit the wire holding the disco ball to the ceiling. The ball fell to the floor and began rolling.

Warren stepped out of the disco ball's way, but then it went right at Ms. Gish. The old teacher ducked under a table, but the ball kept rolling towards Mr. Petrie. The young teacher dodged the ball, then went chasing it out to the hall.

All through this, Tracy kept jerking and shaking around. Susan finally got a good idea. "Pull the plug, Darryl!"

The boy ran over to the sound system and slammed the button again. The music died and the lights came back up.

Darryl rejoined Susan, who watched her friend slowly finish the wild dance. Finally, Tracy stopped moving.

"What is *with* you?" asked Susan.

Tracy was embarrassed beyond belief. "I'm not feeling . . . uh, myself," she squeaked. Then she ran out the doors of the gym.

Chapter 8

Tracy ran down the hallway until she found herself right in front of the girl's washroom. Figuring nobody would find her there, she went inside. Tracy threw water on her face, then paced back and forth for a minute. She looked at herself in the mirror.

"What is happening to me?" said Tracy in despair. "How could I have done that?"

Tracy heard her own voice reply. "You couldn't have. Not without me!"

"Who's that?" Tracy cried. "Who's talking?"

"Try turning around, girl."

Tracy froze for a moment, then slowly began turning. In the mirror, she could see the entire image on the back of her jacket.

"Bet you didn't know you could dance like that!" the image smirked.

Jumping backwards, Tracy tried to get the jacket off. It was no use. The strange fabric stuck to her like glue. Tracy was still wrestling with herself when Warren burst in through the door.

"Tracy! I could hear you out in the hall," he explained. "What's the matter?"

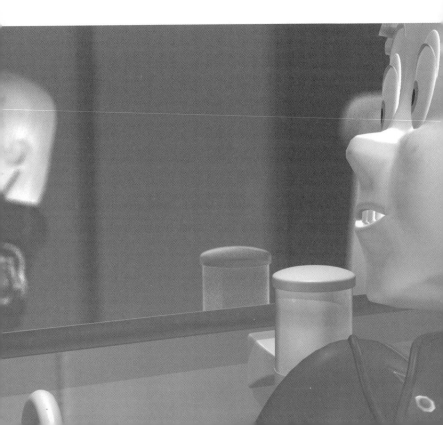

"Just help me!" his sister cried as she struggled with the jacket.

"How?"

"Help me get this jacket off. It's . . . it's stuck . . . and it's alive!"

"I know," Warren told her. "Johnny and I saw the face!"

"What's the fuss, girl?" said the face, still grinning. "You got everything you wanted, didn't you? You danced. You got the guy interested. You got it all."

Tracy ignored the face. "Warren, I've got to get this off. Maybe some monster strength will do it."

Looking around, Tracy spotted the soap dispenser. She squirted out a blob of pink soap and worked it until she had a handful of suds. Tracy held her hand up near Warren's face and blew the bubbles right up his nose.

Warren's sensitive nose immediately began twitching.

"Ah . . . ah . . . ah-choo!"

Warren let out a huge sneeze. He flashed brightly, then grew huge and blue. There were sparkles in the air . . . and Warren became a big blue monster.

"Now *that* should help," Tracy told her brother.

The jacket chuckled. "Who's the big blue ape?"

The Monster ignored the insult. He grabbed Tracy's jacket and picked her up along with it, one hand on each arm. Wrestling with the fabric, the Monster put all of his strength into tearing the jacket off his sister.

"Ouch!" Tracy cried.

"Sorry, Tracy. It just won't budge."

Suddenly, Johnny became visible beside the Monster. "That's a magic jacket, kids. There's only one way to get rid of it."

"Of course," said Tracy. "We need the Book of Spells and the Jewel of Fenrath!"

"Bingo," Johnny agreed. "Then you

just have to reverse the spell and Miss Mouth will be history."

"Haven't you got a house to haunt?" taunted the face on Tracy's jacket.

Johnny shook his head. "Stuff a sock in it." Then he turned back to Tracy and the Monster. "I'll go grab the book and jewel and bring them back. You two try to stay put." The ghost disappeared into thin air as he floated away.

Now that the kids were alone, Tracy turned to her monster brother.

"I guess Johnny was right all along. I should never have used the book and jewel for this. Darryl and Susan will probably never speak to me again," Tracy sighed.

"Yes, they will," said the Monster. "They're your friends."

"Who'd want to be my friend now?" the girl wondered.

"Good question," snapped the jacket. "Without me, you're nothing."

"Don't believe that mouthpiece," the Monster told her. "You're super, Tracy. Anybody would want to be your friend."

Tracy managed a smile. "Thanks. You're a good brother."

The jacket groaned. "It's a good thing we're already in a washroom. I think I'm going to be sick! Enough of this garbage. Let's go dance!"

Tracy yelped as the jacket yanked her to her feet. The crazy coat forced her out the door and back towards the gym. The Monster ran after her.

"Tracy!" he shouted.

Tracy was being pushed quickly to the gym.

"No!" she shouted as she struggled with the jacket. "Not in there. You've already made a fool of me once."

The face on the jacket laughed at her. "Time for you to learn some new steps, girl."

Just as Tracy was about to get dragged

into the gym, she managed to put her hands out and grab the edge of the door.

"Take your hands off the door!" shouted the furious face.

"Try and make me!" came Tracy's determined reply.

The girl and jacket struggled, but it was no use. Finger by finger, Tracy was losing her grip on the door. Just as her last finger gave way, the Monster grabbed her from behind.

"Come on! We can't wait for Johnny," cried the Monster. Picking Tracy up by the shoulders, he raced away from the school.

Chapter 9

Tracy and the Monster were going down the back sidewalks towards home when Tracy thought of something.

"Wait a minute. Johnny told us to stay at school. What if he can't find us out here?"

"Don't worry about it," said the Monster. "He'll find us somehow."

The jacket was whining. "I want to go back to the dance!" Then it jerked Tracy out of the Monster's grip.

Suddenly, Tracy ran to a nearby mailbox. She grabbed it, ripped it off the ground and threw it up in the air.

"Tracy!" cried the Monster. He dashed forward just in time to catch the mailbox.

"It's not me, Warren!" his sister cried desperately.

The jacket dragged the girl to a small car. Tracy grabbed the car and tossed it easily into the air. The Monster had to move fast to catch it before the vehicle smashed on the ground.

Looking around, the Monster spotted Tracy being dragged towards a city bus. Just as she was about to grab the bus and throw it up in the air, the Monster grabbed Tracy by the arms.

"Don't even think about it," he warned the grinning face on the back of the coat.

"You oversized freak!" screamed the jacket. "You . . . you . . . "

Tracy and Monster struggled all the way back home. Of course, it wasn't really Tracy putting up the fuss. Still, the Monster had to keep a tight grip on her. They made it all the way to their back-yard before Tracy broke out of the Monster's grasp again.

"I'm going back to the dance!" screamed the jacket. "I'm going to go wild!"

Tracy started running towards the gate leading out of the yard. Blue lightning leapt from her fingertips, chewing up her mother's garden.

"Warren!" Tracy called to the Monster. "You have to stop me! What if Mom sees?"

The Monster looked around and tried

to think of something to do. Then he spotted a long, green garden hose. The Monster grabbed it and quickly tied a knot to form a lasso. He swung it around and around above his head, then let it go.

The loop flew over Tracy's head and

settled around her. When it dropped to her feet, the Monster yanked the hose, pulling the lasso tight. His sister fell to the ground with a thump.

The jacket was getting very angry. "Do you think you're a cowboy or something? Do I look like a steer to you? Let me up this instant!"

"Where's Johnny?" the Monster cried. He couldn't hold Tracy down like this forever.

Chapter 10

Johnny the Ghost had his own set of problems. He'd flown into Tracy's bedroom just as Mrs. Patterson came in the door. She was busy reading a book – *Dr. Spinkleberger's Guide to Teenage Daughters*.

"Here's the chapter I need," Mrs. Patterson said. "'When Your Daughter Talks Back to You'. Let's see what the expert says."

Mrs. Patterson sat down on the chest where Tracy kept the Jewel of Fenrath and the Book of Spells.

Johnny was upset. He needed the jewel and the book in a hurry. But Mrs. Patterson was no speed-reader. It wasn't until she heard Tracy scream that Mrs. Patterson looked up. She went over to the

window where she saw Tracy looped in the garden hose.

"What are you doing?" she yelled out.

"Just practicing for the dance," Tracy replied, even as she struggled with her jacket.

That was all the time that Johnny needed. He grabbed the book and the jewel, then sailed down to the garden.

"Looks like I got here just in time," he told the kids. "But your mother won't be too happy about her flowers."

"That's the least of our problems," Tracy replied. "I'll hold the jewel and you can read the spell. It's on page one . . ."

The jacket was still fighting Tracy. One of its sleeves got stuck right in her mouth. It was all she could do to spit it out.

" . . . one twenty one!" Tracy finished.

As Johnny flipped through the Book of Spells, the jacket forced Tracy to toss the Jewel of Fenrath to the ground.

"Sorry, guys," said Tracy. "It's the jacket!"

The Monster picked up the jewel and gave it back to his sister. Almost before he even let go, Tracy tossed it right back at him. The Monster tossed it back to Tracy who, once again, threw it back at him. This was starting to look like a strange game of hot potato, when Johnny interrupted.

"Time out," he said, snatching the jewel out of the air. Johnny shoved the Book of Spells towards Tracy. "I'll hold the jewel and you read."

Before Tracy could get the book in her hands, she began to spin around. She spun faster and faster, lifting off the

ground. The movement threw the make-shift lasso off of her.

"You're never getting rid of me!" screamed the jacket. "Never!"

Tracy was spinning like a tornado at this point. Blue sparks of lightning shot from all of her limbs. One of these sparks slammed into a nearby tree, ripping it in two. Furniture on the patio lifted off the ground and started flying around the backyard. It was as if a hurricane had struck the town of Pickford.

"Johnny!" cried the Monster. "You're going to have to read the spell! Hurry!"

Johnny looked determined and began to chant the spell. "*Ich stem nimoy . . .* "

Before he could finish, the face on the jacket started singing.

"She'll be coming round the mountain when she comes! She'll be coming round the mountain when she comes!"

Johnny kept trying, "*Ich stem nimoy flannigan ria . . .* "

"Be kind to your fine feathered friends," sang the jacket. Her voice was terrible! It made Warren's trumpet playing sound good. "For a duck may be somebody's uncle!"

The jacket couldn't even get the words to the song right, but that wasn't the big problem. The big problem was how loud the jacket sang. Its noise totally drowned out Johnny, making it impossible for him to cast the spell.

Suddenly, Tracy stopped spinning and began rising straight into the air.

"Aaagh!" she screamed.

The Monster used the moment to grab his sister. Then he covered the face on the coat with his big blue hand.

"What do you think you're doing?" came the muffled voice of the jacket.

"Try the spell again!" shouted the Monster.

Johnny began to chant the spell again.

"Ich stem nimoy flannigan ria non. . . ." The jewel began to glow blue and jumped out of the ghost's hand. *"Racoota ultra chica stitches para tont!"*

Tracy put the finishing touch on the spell. *"Bricken blaxen!"* she cried.

Blue lightning beams shot out of the jewel, streaking towards the girl. Just before they struck, the Monster jumped out of the way.

Tracy was immediately surrounded by bright, blue energy. It was so bright, the Monster and his ghostly friend had to look away. When they turned back to Tracy, the jacket was gone.

Chapter 11

Tracy patted herself down just to be sure the jacket had really disappeared. Then she let out a big sigh of relief.

"We did it!" cried the Monster.

"It's gone all right," said Johnny. "Off to that big dry cleaner in the sky."

"Thanks, you guys," said Tracy. She gave the Monster a big hug.

She looked around the backyard to check the destruction. "Hey, it looks like the reversing spell undid all the damage!"

The Monster's allergies chose that moment to act up. With a huge sneeze caused by the pollen in the air, the Monster changed back to Warren again. Just in time, too. The kids could hear Susan's voice calling for Tracy.

Warren and Johnny exchanged a look and left Tracy alone. Tracy turned to see Susan and Darryl come into the yard.

"There you are!" exclaimed Susan.

"Hi, guys," said Tracy, more than a little embarrassed.

"We've been trying to find you," said Darryl. "You said you were sick and then didn't come back, so we got worried."

"Are you okay?" asked Susan.

Well, thought Tracy, I am now.

Susan looked at her friend. "If you're

okay, then could you teach me that dance you did?"

Tracy stared at Susan like she was from another planet. "What?"

"The one you did in the gym!"

"Yeah," said Darryl. "That was awesome."

"Sorry, guys. I just don't think I can do that dance again," Tracy told them. "I . . . uh, just sort of did it off the top of my head."

"Don't worry," said Darryl. "We can do another dance then."

"You have to come back with us, Tracy," Susan said. "The dance is just starting. It would be so boring without you."

Tracy's smile lit up the backyard. Despite what she had thought, Darryl and Susan both liked Tracy just as she was. They were true friends after all.

"Sure! Let's get going then," said Tracy.

The kids began to leave the yard when Darryl noticed what was missing. "Hey, where's your jacket? Do you want to go and get it?"

"No!" shouted Tracy. Then she lowered her voice. "I mean, I'm fine just the way I am now."

The End

TOP SECRET!

Sneak Preview of New
Monster By Mistake Episodes

Even more all-new monster-iffic episodes of Monster By Mistake are on the way in 2003 and 2004! Here's an inside look at what's ahead for Warren, Tracy and Johnny:

- It promises to be a battle royale when a superstar wrestler comes to town and challenges the Monster to a match at the Pickford arena.

- There's a gorilla on the loose in Pickford, but where did it come from? It's up to the Monster, Tracy and Johnny to catch the gorilla and solve the mystery.

- When making deliveries for a bakery, Warren discovers who robbed the Pickford Savings and Loan. Can the Monster stop the robbers from getting away?

- Warren, Tracy and Johnny visit Fenrath, the home to Gorgool, the Book of Spells and the jewel. In Fenrath, they discover who imprisoned Gorgool in the ball and what they must do to restore order to this magical kingdom.

MONSTER By Mistake! Videos

Six Monster By Mistake home videos are available and more are on the way.

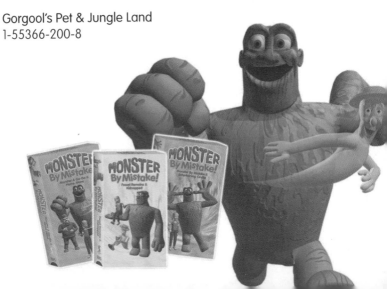

Located in Toronto, Canada, **CCI Entertainment** has been producing quality family entertainment since 1982. Some of their best known shows are "Sharon Lois and Bram's The Elephant Show," "Eric's World," and of course, "Monster By Mistake"!

Catapult Productions in Toronto wants to entertain the whole world with computer animation. Now that we've entertained you, there are only 5 billion people to go!

Mark Mayerson grew up loving animated cartoons and now has a job making them. "Monster By Mistake" is the first TV show he created.

Paul Kropp is an author, editor and educator. His work includes young adult novels, novels for reluctant readers, and the bestselling *How to Make Your Child a Reader for Life*.